THE ADVENTURES OF
DANNY MEADOW MOUSE

Danny popped his head out of another little doorway and laughed at Reddy. *See page 12.*

BURGESS TRADE QUADDIES MARK

The Bedtime Story-Books

THE ADVENTURES OF DANNY MEADOW MOUSE

BY

THORNTON W. BURGESS

Author of "The Adventures of Reddy Fox"
"Old Mother West Wind," etc.

McCLELLAND & STEWART, LIMITED
Publishers   Toronto

PRINTED AND BOUND IN CANADA
T. H. Best Printing Co., Limited, Toronto

CONTENTS

THE ADVENTURES OF
DANNY MEADOW MOUSE

I

DANNY MEADOW MOUSE IS WORRIED

DANNY MEADOW MOUSE sat on his door-step with his chin in his hands, and it was very plain to see that Danny had something on his mind. He had only a nod for Jimmy Skunk, and even Peter Rabbit could get no more than a grumpy "good morning." It wasn't that he had been caught napping the day before by Reddy Fox and nearly made an end of. No, it wasn't that. Danny had learned his lesson, and Reddy would never catch him again.

It wasn't that he was all alone with no one to play with. Danny was rather glad that he was alone. The fact is, Danny Meadow Mouse was worried.

Now worry is one of the worst things in the world, and it didn't seem as if there was anything that Danny Meadow Mouse need worry about. But you know it is the easiest thing in the world to find something to worry over and make yourself uncomfortable about. And when you make yourself uncomfortable, you are almost sure to make every one around you equally uncomfortable. It was so with Danny Meadow Mouse. Striped Chipmunk had twice called him " Cross Patch " that morning, and Johnny Chuck, who had fought Reddy Fox for him the day before, had called him " Grumpy." And what do you think was the matter with Danny Meadow Mouse? Why, he was worrying because

his tail is short. Yes, Sir, that is all that
ailed Danny Meadow Mouse that bright
morning.

You know some people let their looks
make them miserable. They worry because they are homely or freckled, or
short or tall, or thin or stout, all of which
is very foolish. And Danny Meadow
Mouse was just as foolish in worrying
because his tail is short.

It is short! It certainly is all of that!
Danny never had realized how short
until he chanced to meet his cousin
Whitefoot, who lives in the Green Forest.
He was very elegantly dressed, but the
most imposing thing about him was his
long, slim, beautiful tail. Danny had
at once become conscious of his own
stubby little tail, and he had hardly had
pride enough to hold his head up as became an honest Meadow Mouse. Ever
since he had been thinking and thinking,

and wondering how his family came to have such short tails. Then he grew envious and began to wish and wish and wish that he could have a long tail like his cousin Whitefoot.

He was so busy wishing that he had a long tail that he quite forgot to take care of the tail he did have, and he pretty nearly lost it and his life with it. Old Whitetail the Marsh Hawk, spied Danny sitting there moping on his door-step, and came sailing over the tops of the meadow grasses so softly that he all but caught Danny. If it hadn't been for one of the Merry Little Breezes, Danny would have been caught. And all because he was envious. It's a bad, bad habit.

II

DANNY MEADOW MOUSE AND HIS SHORT TAIL

ALL Danny Meadow Mouse could think about was his short tail. He was so ashamed of it that whenever any one passed, he crawled out of sight so that they should not see how short his tail is. Instead of playing in the sunshine as he used to do, he sat and sulked. Pretty soon his friends began to pass without stopping. Finally one day old Mr. Toad sat down in front of Danny and began to ask questions.

" What's the matter? " asked old Mr. Toad.

" Nothing," replied Danny Meadow Mouse.

" I don't suppose that there really is anything the matter, but what do you think is the matter? " said old Mr. Toad.

Danny fidgeted, and old Mr. Toad looked up at jolly, round, red Mr. Sun and winked. " Sun is just as bright as ever, isn't it? " he inquired.

" Yes," said Danny.

" Got plenty to eat and drink, haven't you? " continued Mr. Toad.

" Yes," said Danny.

" Seems to me that that is a pretty good looking suit of clothes you're wearing," said Mr. Toad, eyeing Danny critically. " Sunny weather, plenty to eat and drink, and good clothes — must be you don't know when you're well off, Danny Meadow Mouse."

Danny hung his head. Finally he looked up and caught a kindly twinkle in old Mr. Toad's eyes. " Mr. Toad, how can I get a long tail like my cousin

Whitefoot of the Green Forest?" he asked.

"So that's what's the matter! Ha! ha! ha! Danny Meadow Mouse, I'm ashamed of you! I certainly am ashamed of you!" said Mr. Toad. "What good would a long tail do you? Tell me that."

For a minute Danny didn't know just what to say. "I — I — I'd look so much better if I had a long tail," he ventured.

Old Mr. Toad just laughed. "You never saw a Meadow Mouse with a long tail, did you? Of course not. What a sight it would be! Why, everybody on the Green Meadows would laugh themselves sick at the sight! You see you need to be slim and trim and handsome to carry a long tail well. And then what a nuisance it would be! You would always have to be thinking of your tail and taking care to keep it out of harm's

way. Look at me. I'm homely. Some
folks call me ugly to look at. But no one
tries to catch me as Farmer Brown's
boy does Billy Mink because of his fine
coat; and no one wants to put me in a
cage because of a fine voice. I am satisfied to be just as I am, and if you'll take
my advice, Danny Meadow Mouse, you'll
be satisfied to be just as you are."

"Perhaps you are right," said Danny
Meadow Mouse after a little. "I'll try."

III

DANNY MEADOW MOUSE PLAYS HIDE AND SEEK

LIFE is always a game of hide and seek to Danny Meadow Mouse. You see, he is such a fat little fellow that there are a great many other furry-coated people, and almost as many who wear feathers, who would gobble Danny up for breakfast or for dinner if they could. Some of them pretend to be his friends, but Danny always keeps his eyes open when they are around and always begins to play hide and seek. Peter Rabbit and Jimmy Skunk and Striped Chipmunk and Happy Jack Squirrel are all friends whom he can trust, but he always has a bright twinkling eye open for Reddy Fox and Billy Mink and Shadow the Weasel and old Whitetail the Marsh Hawk, and several more, especially Hooty the Owl at night.

Now Danny Meadow Mouse is a stout-hearted little fellow, and when rough Brother North Wind came shouting across the Green Meadows, tearing to pieces the snow clouds and shaking out the snowflakes until they covered the Green Meadows deep, deep, deep, Danny just snuggled down in his warm coat in his snug little house of grass and waited. Danny liked the snow. Yes, Sir, Danny Meadow Mouse liked the snow. He just loved to dig in it and make tunnels. Through those tunnels in every direction he could go where he pleased and when he pleased without being seen by anybody. It was great fun!

Every little way he made a little round doorway up beside a stiff stalk of grass. Out of this he could peep at the white world, and he could get the fresh cold air. Sometimes, when he was quite sure that no one was around, he would scamper across on top of the snow from one doorway to another, and when he did this, he made the prettiest little footprints.

Now Reddy Fox knew all about those doorways and who made them. Reddy was having hard work to get enough to eat this cold weather, and he was hungry most of the time. One morning, as he came tiptoeing softly over the meadows, what should he see just ahead of him but the head of Danny Meadow Mouse pop out of one of those little round doorways. Reddy's mouth watered, and he stole forward more softly than ever. When he got within jumping distance, he drew his stout hind legs under him and made ready to spring. Presto! Danny Meadow Mouse had disappeared! Reddy Fox jumped just the same and began to dig as fast as he could make his paws go. He could smell Danny Meadow Mouse and that made him almost frantic.

All the time Danny Meadow Mouse was scurrying along one of his little tunnels, and when finally Reddy Fox stopped digging because he was quite out of breath, Danny popped his head out of another little doorway and laughed at Reddy. Of course Reddy saw him, and of course Reddy tried to catch him there, and dug frantically just as before. And of course Danny Meadow Mouse wasn't there.

After a while Reddy Fox grew tired of this kind of a game and tried another plan. The next time he saw Danny Meadow Mouse stick his head out, Reddy

pretended not to see him. He stretched
himself out on the ground and made believe that he was very tired and sleepy.
He closed his eyes. Then he opened them
just the tiniest bit, so that he could see
Danny Meadow Mouse and yet seem to
be asleep. Danny watched him for a
long time. Then he chuckled to himself
and dropped out of sight.

No sooner was he gone than Reddy
Fox stole over close to the little doorway
and waited. "He'll surely stick his head
out again to see if I'm asleep, and then
I'll have him," said Reddy to himself.
So he waited and waited and waited.
By and by he turned his head. There
was Danny Meadow Mouse at another
little doorway laughing at him!

IV

DANNY MEADOW MOUSE had
not enjoyed anything so much
for a long time as he did that
game of hide and seek. He tickled and
chuckled all the afternoon as he thought
about it. Of course Reddy had been
" it." He had been " it " all the time,
for never once had he caught Danny
Meadow Mouse. If he had — well, there
wouldn't have been any more stories
about Danny Meadow Mouse, because
there wouldn't have been any Danny
Meadow Mouse any more.

But Danny never let himself think
about this. He had enjoyed the game all

the more because it had been such a dangerous game. It had been such fun to dive into one of his little round doorways in the snow, run along one of his own little tunnels, and then peep out at another doorway and watch Reddy Fox digging as fast as ever he could at the doorway Danny had just left. Finally Reddy had given up in disgust and gone off muttering angrily to try to find something else for dinner. Danny had sat up on the snow and watched him go. In his funny little squeaky voice Danny shouted:

"Though Reddy Fox is smart and sly,
   Hi-hum-diddle-de-o!
I'm just as smart and twice as spry.
   Hi-hum-diddle-de-o!"

That night Reddy Fox told old Granny Fox all about how he had tried to catch Danny Meadow Mouse. Granny listened with her head cocked on one side.

When Reddy told how fat Danny Meadow Mouse was, her mouth watered. You see now that snow covered the Green Meadows and the Green Forest, Granny and Reddy Fox had hard work to get enough to eat, and they were hungry most of the time.

" I'll go with you down on the meadows to-morrow morning, and then we'll see if Danny Meadow Mouse is as smart as he thinks he is," said Granny Fox.

So, bright and early the next morning, old Granny Fox and Reddy Fox went down on the meadows where Danny Meadow Mouse lives. Danny had felt in his bones that Reddy would come back, so he was watching, and he saw them as soon as they came out of the Green Forest. When he saw old Granny Fox, Danny's heart beat a little faster than before, for he knew that Granny

Fox is very smart and very wise and has learned most of the tricks of all the other little meadow and forest people.

" This is going to be a more exciting game than the other," said Danny to himself, and scurried down out of sight to see that all his little tunnels were clear so that he could run fast through them if he had to. Then he peeped out of one of his little doorways hidden in a clump of tall grass.

Old Granny Fox set Reddy to hunting for Danny's little round doorways, and as fast as he found them, Granny came up and sniffed at each. She knew that she could tell by the smell which one he had been at last. Finally she came straight towards the tall bunch of grass. Danny ducked down and scurried along one of his little tunnels. He heard Granny Fox sniff at the doorway he had just left. Suddenly something plunged

down through the snow right at his very
heels.   Danny didn't have to look to
know that it was Granny Fox herself,
and he squeaked with fright.

V

WHAT HAPPENED ON THE GREEN MEADOWS

THICK and fast things were happening to Danny Meadow Mouse
down on the snow-covered Green
Meadows. Rather, they were almost
happening. He hadn't minded when
Reddy Fox all alone tried to catch him.
Indeed, he had made a regular game of
hide and seek of it and had enjoyed it
immensely. But now it was different.
Granny Fox wasn't so easily fooled as
Reddy Fox. Just Granny alone would
have made the game dangerous for
Danny Meadow Mouse. But Reddy was
with her, and so Danny had two to look
out for, and he got so many frights that

it seemed to him as if his heart had
moved right up into his mouth and was
going to stay there. Yes, Sir, that is just
how it seemed.

Down in his little tunnels underneath
the snow Danny Meadow Mouse felt
perfectly safe from Reddy Fox, who
would stop and dig frantically at the
little round doorway where he had last
seen Danny. But old Granny Fox knew
all about those little tunnels, and she
didn't waste any time digging at the
doorways. Instead she cocked her sharp
little ears and listened with all her might.
Now Granny Fox has very keen ears, oh,
very keen ears, and she heard just what
she hoped she would hear. She heard
Danny Meadow Mouse running along
one of his little tunnels under the snow.

Plunge! Old Granny Fox dived right
into the snow and right through into the
tunnel of Danny Meadow Mouse. Her

two black paws actually touched Danny's tail. He was glad then that it was no longer.

" Ha! " cried Granny Fox, " I almost got him that time! "

Then she ran ahead a little way over the snow, listening as before. Plunge! Into the snow she went again. It was lucky for him that Danny had just turned into another tunnel, for otherwise she would surely have caught him.

Granny Fox blew the snow out of her nose. " Next time I'll get him! " said she.

Now Reddy Fox is quick to learn, especially when it is a way to get something to eat. He watched Granny Fox, and when he understood what she was doing, he made up his mind to have a try himself, for he was afraid that if she caught Danny Meadow Mouse, she would think that he was not big enough to divide. Perhaps that was because Reddy is very selfish himself. So the next time Granny plunged into the snow and missed Danny Meadow Mouse just as before, Reddy rushed in ahead of her, and the minute he heard Danny running down below, he plunged in just as he had seen Granny do. But he didn't take the pains to make sure of just where Danny was, and so of course he didn't come anywhere near him. But he frightened Danny still more and made old Granny Fox lose her temper.

Poor Danny Meadow Mouse! He had never been so frightened in all his life. He didn't know which way to turn or where to run. And so he sat still, which, although he didn't know it, was the very best thing he could do. When he sat still he made no noise, and so of course Granny and Reddy Fox could not tell where he was. Old Granny Fox sat and listened and listened and listened, and

wondered where Danny Meadow Mouse
was. And down under the snow Danny
Meadow Mouse sat and listened and listened and listened, and wondered where
Granny and Reddy Fox were.

"Pooh!" said Granny Fox after a
while, "that Meadow Mouse thinks he
can fool me by sitting still. I'll give him
a scare."

Then she began to plunge into the
snow this way and that way, and sure
enough, pretty soon she landed so close
to Danny Meadow Mouse that one of
her claws scratched him.

VI

DANNY MEADOW MOUSE REMEMBERS AND REDDY FOX FORGETS

"THERE he goes!" cried old Granny Fox. "Don't let him sit still again!"

"I hear him!" shouted Reddy Fox, and plunged down into the snow just as Granny Fox had done a minute before. But he didn't catch anything, and when he had blown the snow out of his nose and wiped it out of his eyes, he saw Granny Fox dive into the snow with no better luck.

"Never mind," said Granny Fox, "as long as we keep him running, we can hear him, and some one of these times we'll catch him. Pretty soon he'll get too

tired to be so spry, and when he is — "
Granny didn't finish, but licked her
chops and smacked her lips. Reddy Fox
grinned, then licked his chops and
smacked his lips. Then once more they
took turns diving into the snow.

And down underneath in the little
tunnels he had made, Danny Meadow
Mouse was running for his life. He was
getting tired, just as old Granny Fox had
said he would. He was almost out of
breath. He was sore and one leg smarted,
for in one of her jumps old Granny Fox
had so nearly caught him that her claws
had torn his pants and scratched him.

"Oh, dear! Oh, dear! If only I had
time to think!" panted Danny Meadow
Mouse, and then he squealed in still
greater fright as Reddy Fox crashed
down into his tunnel right at his very
heels. "I've got to get somewhere! I've
got to get somewhere where they can't

get at me! " he sobbed. And right that very instant he remembered the old fence-post!

The old fence-post lay on the ground and was hollow. Fastened to it were long wires with sharp cruel barbs. Danny had made a tunnel over to that old fence-post the very first day after the snow came, for in that hollow in the old post he had a secret store of seeds. Why hadn't he thought of it before? It must have been because he was too frightened to think. But he remembered now, and he dodged into the tunnel that led to the old fence-post, running faster than ever, for though his heart was in his mouth from fear, in his heart was hope, and hope is a wonderful thing.

Now old Granny Fox knew all about that old fence-post and she remembered all about those barbed wires fastened to it. Although they were covered with snow she knew just about where they lay, and just before she reached them she stopped plunging down into the snow. Reddy Fox knew about those wires, too, but he was so excited that he forgot all about them.

"Stop!" cried old Granny Fox sharply.

But Reddy Fox didn't hear, or if he heard he didn't heed. His sharp ears could hear Danny Meadow Mouse running almost underneath him. Granny Fox could stop if she wanted to, but he was going to have Danny Meadow Mouse for his breakfast! Down into the snow he plunged as hard as ever he could.

"Oh! Oh! Wow! Wow! Oh, dear! Oh, dear!"

That wasn't the voice of Danny Meadow Mouse. Oh, my, no! It was the voice of Reddy Fox. Yes, Sir, it was the voice of Reddy Fox. He had landed with one of his black paws right on one of those sharp wire barbs, and it did hurt dreadfully.

"I never did know a young Fox who could get into so much trouble as you can!" snapped old Granny Fox. as Reddy hobbled along on three legs behind her, across the snow-covered Greer Meadows. "It serves you right for forgetting!"

"Yes'm," said Reddy meekly.

And safe in the hollow of the old fence-post, Danny Meadow Mouse was dressing the scratch on his leg made by the claws of old Granny Fox.

VII

OLD Granny Fox kept thinking about Danny Meadow Mouse. She knew that he was fat, and it made her mouth water every time she thought of him. She made up her mind that she must and would have him. She knew that Danny had been very, very much frightened when she and Reddy Fox had tried so hard to catch him by plunging down through the snow into his little tunnels after him, and she felt pretty sure that he wouldn't go far away from the old fence-post, in the hollow of which he was snug and safe.

Old Granny Fox is very smart. "Danny Meadow Mouse won't put his

nose out of that old fence-post for a day
or two. Then he'll get tired of staying
inside all the time, and he'll peep out of
one of his little round doorways to see
if the way is clear. If he doesn't see any
danger, he'll come out and run around
on top of the snow to get some of the
seeds in the tops of the tall grasses that
stick out through the snow. If nothing
frightens him, he'll keep going a little
farther and a little farther from that old
fence-post. I must see to it that Danny
Meadow Mouse isn't frightened for a
few days." So said old Granny Fox to
herself, as she lay under a hemlock-tree,
studying how she could best get the
next meal.

Then she called Reddy Fox to her and
forbade him to go down on the meadows
until she should tell him he might.
Reddy grumbled and mumbled and didn't
see why he shouldn't go where he pleased,

but he didn't dare disobey. You see he had a sore foot. He had hurt it on a wire barb when he was plunging through the snow after Danny Meadow Mouse, and now he had to run on three legs. That meant that he must depend upon Granny Fox to help him get enough to eat. So Reddy didn't dare to disobey.

It all came out just as Granny Fox had thought it would. Danny Meadow Mouse *did* get tired of staying in the old fence-post. He *did* peep out first, and then he *did* run a little way on the snow, and then a little farther and a little farther. But all the time he took great care not to get more than a jump or two from one of his little round doorways leading down to his tunnels under the snow.

Hidden on the edge of the Green Forest, Granny Fox watched him. She looked up at the sky, and she knew that it was going to snow again. "That's good," said she. "To-morrow morning I'll have fat Meadow Mouse for breakfast," and she smiled a hungry smile.

The next morning, before jolly, round, red Mr. Sun was out of bed, old Granny Fox trotted down on to the meadows and straight over to where, down under the snow, lay the old fence-post. It had snowed again, and all of the little doorways of Danny Meadow Mouse were covered up with soft, fleecy snow. Behind Granny Fox limped Reddy Fox, grumbling to himself.

When they reached the place where the old fence-post lay buried under the snow, old Granny Fox stretched out as flat as she could. Then she told Reddy to cover her up with the new soft snow. Reddy did as he was told, but all the time he grumbled. "Now you go off to the Green Forest and keep out of

sight," said Granny Fox. " By and by
I'll bring you some Meadow Mouse for
your breakfast," and Granny Fox
chuckled to think how smart she was
and how she was going to catch Danny
Meadow Mouse.

VIII

BROTHER NORTH WIND PROVES A FRIEND

DANNY MEADOW MOUSE had seen nothing of old Granny Fox or Reddy Fox for several days. Every morning the first thing he did, even before he had breakfast, was to climb up to one of his little round doorways and peep out over the beautiful white meadows, to see if there was any danger near. But every time he did this, Danny used a different doorway. "For," said Danny to himself, "if any one should happen, just happen, to see me this morning, they might be waiting just outside my doorway to catch me to-morrow morning." You see there is a great deal of wisdom in the little head that Danny Meadow Mouse carries on his shoulders.

But the first day and the second day and the third day he saw nothing of old Granny Fox or of Reddy Fox, and he began to enjoy running through his tunnels under the snow and scurrying across from one doorway to another on top of the snow, just as he had before the Foxes had tried so hard to catch him. But he hadn't forgotten, as Granny Fox had hoped he would. No, indeed, Danny Meadow Mouse hadn't forgotten. He was too wise for that.

One morning, when he started to climb up to one of his little doorways, he found that it was closed. Yes, Sir, it was closed. In fact, there wasn't any doorway. More snow had fallen from the clouds in the night and had covered up every one of the little round doorways of Danny Meadow Mouse.

"Ha!" said Danny, "I shall have a busy day, a very busy day, opening all my doorways. I'll eat my breakfast, and then I'll go to work."

So Danny Meadow Mouse ate a good breakfast of seeds which he had stored in the hollow in the old fence-post buried under the snow, and then he began work on the nearest doorway. It really wasn't work at all, for you see the snow was soft and light, and Danny dearly loved to dig in it. In a few minutes he had made a wee hole through which he could peep up at jolly, round Mr. Sun. In a few minutes more he had made it big enough to put his head out. He looked this way and he looked that way. Far, far off on the top of a tree he could see old Roughleg the Hawk, but he was so far away that Danny didn't fear him at all.

"I don't see anything or anybody to

be afraid of," said Danny and poked his head out a little farther.

Then he sat and studied everything around him a long, long time. It was a beautiful white world, a very beautiful white world. Everything was so white and pure and beautiful that it didn't seem possible that harm or danger for any one could even be thought of. But Danny Meadow Mouse learned long ago that things are not always what they seem, and so he sat with just his little head sticking out of his doorway and studied and studied. Just a little way off was a little heap of snow.

" I don't remember that," said Danny. " And I don't remember anything that would make that. There isn't any little bush or old log or anything underneath it. Perhaps rough Brother North Wind heaped it up, just for fun."

But all the time Danny Meadow

Mouse kept studying and studying that little heap of snow. Pretty soon he saw rough Brother North Wind coming his way and tossing the snow about as he came. He caught a handful from the top of the little heap of snow that Danny was studying, and when he had passed, Danny's sharp eyes saw something red there. It was just the color of the cloak old Granny Fox wears.

> " Granny Fox, you can't fool me!
> I see you plain as plain can be! "

shouted Danny Meadow Mouse and dropped down out of sight, while old Granny Fox shook the snow from her red cloak and, with a snarl of disappointment and anger, slowly started for the Green Forest, where Reddy Fox was waiting for her.

IX

DANNY MEADOW MOUSE IS CAUGHT AT LAST

" Tippy-toppy-tippy-toe,
　　Play and frolic in the snow!
　　Now you see me!　Now you don't!
　　Think you'll catch me, but you won't!
　　Tippy-toppy-tippy-toe,
　　Oh, such fun to play in snow! "

DANNY MEADOW MOUSE sang
this, or at least he tried to sing
it, as he skipped about on the
snow that covered the Green Meadows.
But Danny Meadow Mouse has such a
little voice, such a funny little squeaky
voice, that had you been there you probably would never have guessed that he
was singing.　He thought he was, though,
and was enjoying it just as much as if

he had the most beautiful voice in the
world. You know singing is nothing in
the world but happiness in the heart
making itself heard.

Oh, yes, Danny Meadow Mouse was
happy! Why shouldn't he have been?
Hadn't he proved himself smarter than
old Granny Fox? That is something to
make any one happy. Some folks may
fool Granny Fox once; some may fool
her twice; but there are very few who
can keep right on fooling her until she
gives up in disgust. That is just what
Danny Meadow Mouse had done, and
he felt very smart and of course he felt
very happy.

So Danny sang his little song and
skipped about in the moonlight, and
dodged in and out of his little round
doorways, and all the time kept his
sharp little eyes open for any sign of
Granny Fox or Reddy Fox. But with

all his smartness, Danny forgot. Yes,
Sir, Danny forgot one thing. He forgot
to watch up in the sky. He knew that
of course old Roughleg the Hawk was
asleep, so he had nothing to fear from
him. But he never once thought of
Hooty the Owl.

Dear me, dear me! Forgetting is a
dreadful habit. If nobody ever forgot,
there wouldn't be nearly so much trouble
in the world. No, indeed, there wouldn't
be nearly so much trouble. And Danny
Meadow Mouse forgot. He skipped and
sang and was happy as could be, and never
once thought to watch up in the sky.

Over in the Green Forest Hooty the
Owl had had poor hunting, and he was
feeling cross. You see, Hooty was hungry, and hunger is apt to make one feel
cross. The longer he hunted, the hun-
grier and crosser he grew. Suddenly he
thought of Danny Meadow Mouse.

"I suppose he is asleep somewhere safe and snug under the snow," grumbled Hooty, "but he might be, he just *might* be out for a frolic in the moonlight. I believe I'll go down on the meadows and see."

Now Hooty the Owl can fly without making the teeniest, weeniest sound. It seems as if he just drifts along through the air like a great shadow. Now he spread his great wings and floated out over the meadows. You know Hooty can see as well at night as most folks can by day, and it was not long before he saw Danny Meadow Mouse skipping about on the snow and dodging in and out of his little round doorways. Hooty's great eyes grew brighter and fiercer. Without a sound he floated through the moonlight until he was just over Danny Meadow Mouse.

Too late Danny looked up. His little

song ended in a tiny squeak of fear, and
he started for his nearest little round
doorway. Hooty the Owl reached down
with his long cruel claws and — Danny
Meadow Mouse was caught at last!

X

A STRANGE RIDE AND HOW IT ENDED

DANNY MEADOW MOUSE often had sat watching Skimmer the Swallow sailing around up in the blue, blue sky. He had watched Ol' Mistah Buzzard go up, up, up, until he was nothing but a tiny speck, and Danny had wondered how it would seem to be way up above the Green Meadows and the Green Forest and look down. It had seemed to him that it must be very wonderful and beautiful. Sometimes he had wished that he had wings and could go up in the air and look down. And now here he was, he, Danny Meadow Mouse, actually doing that very thing!

But Danny could see nothing wonder-

ful or beautiful now. No, indeed!
Everything was terrible, for you see
Danny Meadow Mouse wasn't flying
himself. He was being carried. Yes,
Sir, Danny Meadow Mouse was being
carried through the air in the cruel
claws of Hooty the Owl! And all because Danny had forgotten — forgotten
to watch up in the sky for danger.

Poor, poor Danny Meadow Mouse!
Hooty's great cruel claws hurt him
dreadfully! But it wasn't the pain that
was the worst. No, indeed! It wasn't
the pain! It was the thought of what
would happen when Hooty reached his
home in the Green Forest, for he knew
that there Hooty would gobble him up,
bones and all. As he flew, Hooty kept
chuckling, and Danny Meadow Mouse
knew just what those chuckles meant.
They meant that Hooty was thinking
of the good meal he was going to have.

Hanging there in Hooty's great cruel claws, Danny looked down on the snow-covered Green Meadows he loved so well. They seemed a frightfully long way below him, though really they were not far at all, for Hooty was flying very low. But Danny Meadow Mouse had never in all his life been so high up before, and so it seemed to him that he was way, way up in the sky, and he shut his eyes so as not to see. But he couldn't keep them shut. No, Sir, he couldn't keep them shut! He just *had* to keep opening them. There was the dear old Green Forest drawing nearer and nearer. It always had looked very beautiful to Danny Meadow Mouse, but now it looked terrible, very terrible indeed, because over in it, in some dark place, was the home of Hooty the Owl.

Just ahead of him was the Old Briar-patch where Peter Rabbit lives so safely.

Every old bramble in it was covered
with snow and it was very, very beautiful. Really everything was just as beautiful as ever — the moonlight, the Green
Forest, the snow-covered Green Meadows, the Old Briar-patch. The only
change was in Danny Meadow Mouse
himself, and it was all because he had
forgotten.

Suddenly Danny began to wriggle and
struggle. "Keep still!" snapped Hooty
the Owl.

But Danny only struggled harder than
ever. It seemed to him that Hooty
wasn't holding him as tightly as at first.
He felt one of Hooty's claws slip. It
tore his coat and hurt dreadfully, but it
slipped! The fact is, Hooty had only
grabbed Danny Meadow Mouse by the
loose part of his coat, and up in the air
he couldn't get hold of Danny any
better. Danny kicked, squirmed and

twisted, and twisted, squirmed, and
kicked. He felt his coat tear and of
course the skin with it, but he kept right
on, for now he was hanging almost free.
Hooty had started down now, so as to
get a better hold. Danny gave one
more kick and then — he felt himself
falling!

Danny Meadow Mouse shut his eyes
and held his breath. Down, down, down
he fell. It seemed to him that he never
would strike the snow-covered meadows!
Really he fell only a very little distance.
But it seemed a terrible distance to
Danny. He hit something that scratched
him, and then plump! he landed in the
soft snow right in the very middle of the
Old Briar-patch, and the last thing he
remembered was hearing the scream of
disappointment and rage of Hooty the
Owl.

XI

PETER RABBIT GETS A FRIGHT

PETER RABBIT sat in his favorite place in the middle of the dear Old Briar-patch, trying to decide which way he would go on his travels that night. The night before he had had a narrow escape from old Granny Fox over in the Green Forest. There was nothing to eat around the Smiling Pool and no one to talk to there any more, and you know that Peter must either eat or ask questions in order to be perfectly happy. No, the Smiling Pool was too dull a place to interest Peter on such a beautiful moonlight night, and Peter had no mind to try his legs against those

of old Granny Fox again in the Green
Forest.

Early that morning, just after Peter
had settled down for his morning nap,
Tommy Tit the Chickadee had dropped
into the dear Old Briar-patch just to be
neighborly. Peter was just dozing off
when he heard the cheeriest little voice
in the world. It was saying:

" Dee-dee-chickadee!
I see you! Can you see me? "

Peter began to smile even before he
could get his eyes open and look up.
There, right over his head, was Tommy
Tit hanging head down from a nodding
old bramble. In a twinkling he was
down on the snow right in front of Peter,
then up in the brambles again, right side
up, upside down, here, there, every-
where, never still a minute, and all the
time chattering away in the cheeriest
little voice in the world.

" Dee-dee-chickadee!
I'm as happy as can be!
Find it much the better way
To be happy all the day.
Dee-dee-chickadee!
Everybody's good to me! "

" Hello, Tommy! " said Peter Rabbit.
" Where'd you come from? "

" From Farmer Brown's new orchard
up on the hill. It's a fine orchard, Peter
Rabbit, a fine orchard. I go there every
morning for my breakfast. If the winter
lasts long enough, I'll have all the trees
cleaned up for Farmer Brown."

Peter looked puzzled. " What do you
mean? " he asked.

" Just what I say," replied Tommy Tit,
almost turning a somersault in the air.
" There's a million eggs of insects on
those young peach-trees, but I'm clearing
them all off as fast as I can. They're
mighty fine eating, Peter Rabbit, mighty
fine eating! " And with that Tommy

Tit had said good-by and flitted
away.

Peter was thinking of that young
orchard now, as he sat in the moonlight
trying to make up his mind where to go.
The thought of those young peach-trees
made his mouth water. It was a long
way up to the orchard on the hill, a
very long way, and Peter was wondering
if it really was safe to go. He had just
about made up his mind to try it, for
Peter is very, very fond of the bark of
young peach-trees, when thump! something dropped out of the sky at his very
feet.

It startled Peter so that he nearly
tumbled over backward. And right at
the same instant came the fierce, angry
scream of Hooty the Owl. That almost
made Peter's heart stop beating, although he knew that Hooty couldn't get
him down there in the Old Briar-patch.

When Peter got his wits together and his heart didn't go so jumpy, he looked to see what had dropped so close to him out of the sky. His big eyes grew bigger than ever, and he rubbed them to make quite sure that he really saw what he thought he saw. Yes, there was no doubt about it — there at his feet lay Danny Meadow Mouse!

XII

THE OLD BRIAR - PATCH HAS A NEW TENANT

DANNY MEADOW MOUSE slowly opened his eyes and then closed them again quickly, as if afraid to look around. He could hear some one talking. It was a pleasant voice, not at all like the terrible voice of Hooty the Owl, which was the very last thing that Danny Meadow Mouse could remember. Danny lay still a minute and listened.

" Why, Danny Meadow Mouse, where in the world did you drop from? " asked the voice. It sounded like — why, very much like Peter Rabbit speaking. Danny

opened his eyes again.   It *was* Peter
Rabbit.

"Where — where am I? " asked Danny
Meadow Mouse in a very weak and
small voice.

"In the middle of the dear Old Briar-
patch with me," replied Peter Rabbit.
"But how did you get here?   You
seemed to drop right out of the sky."

Danny Meadow Mouse shuddered.
Suddenly he remembered everything:
how Hooty the Owl had caught him in
great cruel claws and had carried him
through the moonlight across the snow-
covered Green Meadows; how he had
felt Hooty's claws slip and then had
struggled and kicked and twisted and
turned until his coat had torn and he
had dropped down, down, down until
he had landed in the soft snow and
knocked all the breath out of his little
body.   The very last thing he could re-

member was Hooty's fierce scream of
rage and disappointment. Danny shuddered again.

Then a new thought came to him. He
must get out of sight! Hooty might
catch him again! Danny tried to
scramble to his feet.

" Ooch! Oh! " groaned Danny and
lay still again.

" There, there. Keep still, Danny
Meadow Mouse. There's nothing to be
afraid of here," said Peter Rabbit gently.
His big eyes filled with tears as he looked
at Danny Meadow Mouse, for Danny
was all torn and hurt by the cruel claws
of Hooty the Owl, and you know Peter
has a very tender heart.

So Danny lay still, and while Peter
Rabbit tried to make him comfortable
and dress his hurts, he told Peter all
about how he had forgotten to watch up
in the sky and so had been caught by

"I tell you what, you stay right here!" *Page 57.*

Hooty the Owl, and all about his terrible ride in Hooty's cruel claws.

" Oh, dear, whatever shall I do now? "
he ended. " However shall I get back
home to my warm house of grass, my
safe little tunnels under the snow, and
my little store of seeds in the snug hollow
in the old fence-post? "

Peter Rabbit looked thoughtful.
" You can't do it," said he. " You
simply can't do it. It is such a long
way for a little fellow like you that it
wouldn't be safe to try. If you went at
night, Hooty the Owl might catch you
again. If you tried in daylight, old
Roughleg the Hawk would be almost
sure to see you. And night or day old
Granny Fox or Reddy Fox might come
snooping around, and if they did, they
would be sure to catch you. I tell you
what, you stay right here! The dear
Old Briar-patch is the safest place in the

world. Why, just think, here you can come out in broad daylight and laugh at Granny and Reddy Fox and at old Roughleg the Hawk, because the good old brambles will keep them out, if they try to get you. You can make just as good tunnels under the snow here as you had there, and there are lots and lots of seeds on the ground to eat. You know I don't care for them myself. I'm lonesome sometimes, living here all alone. You stay here, and we'll have the Old Briar-patch to ourselves."

Danny Meadow Mouse looked at Peter gratefully. " I will, and thank you ever so much, Peter Rabbit," he said.

And this is how the dear Old Briar-patch happened to have another tenant.

XIII

PETER RABBIT VISITS THE PEACH ORCHARD

"DON'T go, Peter Rabbit! Don't go!" begged Danny Meadow Mouse.

Peter hopped to the edge of the Old Briar-patch and looked over the moonlit, snow-covered meadows to the hill back of Farmer Brown's house. On that hill was the young peach orchard of which Tommy Tit the Chickadee had told him, and ever since Peter's mouth had watered and watered every time he thought of those young peach-trees and the tender bark on them.

"I think I will, Danny, just this once," said Peter. "It's a long way, and I've never been there before; but

I guess it's just as safe as the Meadows
or the Green Forest.

> " Oh I'm as bold as bold can be!
>   Sing hoppy-hippy-hippy-hop-o!
> I'll hie me forth the world to see!
>   Sing hoppy-hippy-hippy-hop-o!
>   My ears are long,
>   My legs are strong,
>   So now good day;
>   I'll hie away!
>   Sing hoppy-hippy-hippy-hop-o! "

And with that, Peter Rabbit left the
dear safe Old Briar-patch, and away he
went lipperty-lipperty-lip, across the
Green Meadows towards the hill and the
young orchard back of Farmer Brown's
house.

Danny Meadow Mouse watched him
go and shook his head in disapproval.
" Foolish, foolish, foolish! " he said over
and over to himself. " Why can't Peter
be content with the good things that he
has? "

Peter Rabbit hurried along through the moonlight, stopping every few minutes to sit up to look and listen. He heard the fierce hunting call of Hooty the Owl way over in the Green Forest, so he felt sure that at present there was nothing to fear from him. He knew that since their return to the Green Meadows and the Green Forest, Granny and Reddy Fox had kept away from Farmer Brown's, so he did not worry about them.

All in good time Peter came to the young orchard. It was just as Tommy Tit the Chickadee had told him. Peter hopped up to the nearest peach-tree and nibbled the bark. My, how good it tasted! He went all around the tree, stripping off the bark. He stood up on his long hind legs and reached as high as he could. Then he dug the snow away and ate down as far as he could. When

he could get no more tender young bark,
he went on to the next tree.

Now though Peter didn't know it, he
was in the very worst kind of mischief.
You see, when he took off all the bark
all the way around the young peach-tree
he killed the tree, for you know it is on
the inside of the bark that the sap which
gives life to a tree and makes it grow
goes up from the roots to all the
branches. So when Peter ate the bark
all the way around the trunk of the
young tree, he had made it impossible
for the sap to come up in the spring.
Oh, it was the very worst kind of mischief that Peter Rabbit was in.

But Peter didn't know it, and he kept
right on filling that big stomach of his
and enjoying it so much that he forgot
to watch out for danger. Suddenly,
just as he had begun on another tree, a
great roar right behind him made him

jump almost out of his skin. He knew
that voice, and without waiting to even
look behind him, he started for the
stone wall on the other side of the
orchard. Right at his heels, his great
mouth wide open, was Bowser the
Hound.

XIV

FARMER BROWN SETS A TRAP

PETER RABBIT was in trouble. He had gotten into mischief and now, like every one who gets into mischief, he wished that he hadn't. The worst of it was that he was a long way from his home in the dear Old Briar-patch, and he didn't know how he ever could get back there again. Where was he? Why, in the stone wall on one side of Farmer Brown's young peach orchard. How Peter blessed the old stone wall in which he had found a safe hiding-place! Bowser had hung around nearly all night, so that Peter had not dared to try to go home. Now it was daylight, and

Peter knew it would not be safe to put
his nose outside.

Peter was worried, so worried that he
couldn't go to sleep as he usually does
in the daytime. So he sat hidden in the
old wall and waited and watched. By
and by he saw Farmer Brown and Farmer
Brown's boy come out into the orchard.
Right away they saw the mischief which
Peter had done, and he could tell by the
sound of their voices that they were
very, very angry. They went away,
but before long they were back again,
and all day long Peter watched them
work putting something around each of
the young peach-trees. Peter grew so
curious that he forgot all about his
troubles and how far away from home
he was. He could hardly wait for night
to come so that he might see what they
had been doing.

Just as jolly, round, red Mr. Sun

started to go to bed behind the Purple
Hills, Farmer Brown and his boy started
back to the house. Farmer Brown was
smiling now.

" I guess that that will fix him! " he
said.

" Now what does he mean by that? "
thought Peter. " Who will it fix? Can
it be me? I don't need any fixing."

He waited just as long as he could.
When all was still, and the moonlight
had begun to make shadows of the trees
on the snow, Peter very cautiously crept
out of his hiding-place. Bowser the
Hound was nowhere in sight, and everything was as quiet and peaceful as it had
been when he first came into the orchard
the night before. Peter had fully made
up his mind to go straight home as fast
as his long legs would take him, but his
dreadful curiosity insisted that first he
must find out what Farmer Brown and

his boy had been doing to the young
peach-trees.

So Peter hurried over to the nearest
tree. All around the trunk of the tree,
from the ground clear up higher than
Peter could reach, was wrapped wire
netting. Peter couldn't get so much as
a nibble of the delicious bark. He
hadn't intended to take any, for he had
meant to go right straight home, but
now that he couldn't get any, he wanted
some more than ever, — just a bite.
Peter looked around. Everything was
quiet. He would try the next tree, and
then he would go home.

But the next tree was wrapped with
wire. Peter hesitated, looked around,
turned to go home, thought of how good
that bark had tasted the night before,
hesitated again, and then hurried over
to the third tree. It was protected just
like the others. Then Peter forgot all

about going home. He wanted some
of that delicious bark, and he ran from
one tree to another as fast as he could go.

At last, way down at the end of the
orchard, Peter found a tree that had no
wire around it. " They must have forgotten this one! " he thought, and his
eyes sparkled. All around on the snow
were a lot of little, shiny wires, but
Peter didn't notice them. All he saw
was that delicious bark on the young
peach-tree. He hopped right into the
middle of the wires, and then, just as he
reached up to take the first bite of bark,
he felt something tugging at one of his
hind legs.

XV

PETER RABBIT IS CAUGHT IN A SNARE

WHEN Peter Rabbit, reaching up to nibble the bark of one of Farmer Brown's young trees, felt something tugging at one of his hind legs, he was so startled that he jumped to get away. Instead of doing this, he fell flat on his face. The thing on his hind leg had tightened and held him fast. A great fear came to Peter Rabbit, and lying there in the snow, he kicked and struggled with all his might. But the more he kicked, the tighter grew that hateful thing on his leg! Finally he grew too tired to kick any more and lay still. The dreadful thing that held him

hurt his leg, but it didn't pull when he
lay still.

When he had grown a little calmer,
Peter sat up to examine the thing which
held him so fast. It was something like
one of the blackberry vines he had sometimes tripped over, only it was bright
and shiny, and had no branches or tiny
prickers, and one end was fastened to a
stake. Peter tried to bite off the shiny
thing, but even his great, sharp front
teeth couldn't cut it. Then Peter knew
what it was. It was wire! It was a
snare which Farmer Brown had set to
catch him, and which he had walked
right into because he had been so greedy
for the bark of the young peach-tree
that he had not used his eyes to look out
for danger.

Oh, how Peter Rabbit did wish that
he had not been so curious to know what
Farmer Brown had been doing that day,

and that he had gone straight home as
he had meant to do, instead of trying to
get one more meal of young peach-bark!
Big tears rolled down Peter's cheeks.
What should he do? What *could* he do?
For a long time Peter sat in the moonlight, trying to think of something to do.
At last he thought of the stake to which
that hateful wire was fastened. The
stake was of wood, and Peter's teeth
would cut wood. Peter's heart gave a
great leap of hope, and he began at once
to dig away the snow from around the
stake, and then settled himself to gnaw
the stake in two.

Peter had been hard at work on the
stake a long time and had it a little more
than half cut through, when he heard a
loud sniff down at the other end of the
orchard. He looked up to see — whom
do you think? Why, Bowser the
Hound! He hadn't seen Peter yet, but

he had already found Peter's tracks, and
it wouldn't be but a few minutes before
he found Peter himself.

Poor Peter Rabbit! There wasn't
time to finish cutting off the stake.
What could he do? He made a frightened jump just as he had when he first
felt the wire tugging at his leg. Just as
before, he was thrown flat on his face.
He scrambled to his feet and jumped
again, only to be thrown just as before.
Just then Bowser the Hound saw him
and opening his mouth sent forth a great
roar. Peter made one more frantic
jump. Snap! the stake had broken!
Peter pitched forward on his head, turned
a somersault, and scrambled to his feet.
He was free at last! That is, he could
run, but after him dragged a piece of the
stake.

How Peter did run! It was hard work,
for you know he had to drag that piece

of stake after him. But he did it, and just in time he crawled into the old stone wall on one side of the orchard, while Bowser the Hound barked his disappointment to the moon.

XVI

PETER RABBIT sat in the old stone wall along one side of Farmer Brown's orchard, waiting for Mrs. Moon to put out her light and leave the world in darkness until jolly, round, red Mr. Sun should kick off his rosy bedclothes and begin his daily climb up in the blue, blue sky. In the winter, Mr. Sun is a late sleeper, and Peter knew that there would be two or three hours after Mrs. Moon put out her light when it would be quite dark. And Peter also knew too that by this time Hooty the Owl would probably have caught his dinner. So would old Granny Fox and Reddy Fox. Bowser the Hound

would be too sleepy to be on the watch.
It would be the very safest time for
Peter to try to get to his home in the
dear Old Briar-patch.

So Peter waited and waited. Twice
Bowser the Hound, who had chased
him into the old wall, came over and
barked at him and tried to get at him.
But the old wall kept Peter safe, and
Bowser gave it up. And all the time
Peter sat waiting he was in great pain.
You see that shiny wire was drawn so
tight that it cut into his flesh and hurt
dreadfully, and to the other end of the
wire was fastened a piece of wood, part
of the stake to which the snare had been
made fast and which Peter had managed
to gnaw and break off.

It was on account of this that Peter
was waiting for Mrs. Moon to put out
her light. He knew that with that stake
dragging after him he would have to go

very slowly, and he could not run any more risk of danger than he actually had to. So he waited and waited, and by and by, sure enough, Mrs. Moon put out her light. Peter waited a little longer, listening with all his might. Everything was still. Then Peter crept out of the old stone wall.

Right away trouble began. The stake dragging at the end of the wire fast to his leg caught among the stones and pulled Peter up short. My, how it did hurt! It made the tears come. But Peter shut his teeth hard, and turning back, he worked until he got the stake free. Then he started on once more, dragging the stake after him.

Very slowly across the orchard and under the fence on the other side crept Peter Rabbit, his leg so stiff and sore that he could hardly touch it to the snow, and all the time dragging that

piece of stake, which seemed to grow
heavier and harder to drag every minute. Peter did not dare to go out across
the open fields, for fear some danger
might happen along, and he would have
no place to hide. So he crept along
close to the fences where bushes grow,
and this made it very, very hard, for the
dragging stake was forever catching in
the bushes with a yank at the sore leg
which brought Peter up short with a
squeal of pain.

This was bad enough, but all the time
Peter was filled with a dreadful fear
that Hooty the Owl or Granny Fox
might just happen along. He had to
stop to rest very, very often, and then
he would listen and listen. Over and
over again he said to himself:

"Oh, dear, whatever did I go up to
the young peach orchard for when I
knew I had no business there? Why

couldn't I have been content with all
the good things that were mine in the
Green Forest and on the Green Meadows? Oh, dear! Oh, dear! "

Just as jolly, round, red Mr. Sun began
to light up the Green Meadows, Peter
Rabbit reached the dear Old Briar-
patch. Danny Meadow Mouse was sitting on the edge of it anxiously watching
for him. Peter crawled up and started
to creep in along one of his little private
paths. He got in himself, but the dragging stake caught among the brambles,
and Peter just fell down in the snow
right where he was, too tired and worn
out to move.

XVII

DANNY MEADOW MOUSE BECOMES WORRIED

DANNY MEADOW MOUSE limped around through the dear Old Briar-patch, where he had lived with Peter Rabbit ever since he had squirmed out of the claws of Hooty the Owl and dropped there, right at the feet of Peter Rabbit. Danny limped because he was still lame and sore from Hooty's terrible claws, but he didn't let himself think much about that, because he was so thankful to be alive at all. So he limped around in the Old Briar-patch, picking up seed which had fallen on the snow, and sometimes pulling down a few of the red berries which cling all winter to the wild rose bushes. The

seeds in these were very nice indeed, and
Danny always felt especially good after
a meal of them.

Danny Meadow Mouse had grown
very fond of Peter Rabbit, for Peter had
been very, very good to him. Danny
felt that he never, never could repay
all of Peter's kindness. It had been
very good of Peter to offer to share the
Old Briar-patch with Danny, because
Danny was so far from his own home
that it would not be safe for him to try
to get back there. But Peter had done
more than that. He had taken care
of Danny, such good care, during the
first few days after Danny's escape
from Hooty the Owl. He had brought
good things to eat while Danny was too
weak and sore to get things for himself.
Oh, Peter had been very good indeed to
him!

But now, as Danny limped around, he

was not happy. No, Sir, he was not
happy. The truth is, Danny Meadow
Mouse was worried. It was a different
kind of worry from any he had known
before. You see, for the first time in his
life, Danny was worrying about some
one else. He was worrying about Peter
Rabbit. Peter had been gone from the
Old Briar-patch a whole night and a
whole day. He often was gone all night,
but never all day too. Danny was sure
that something had happened to Peter.
He thought of how he had begged
Peter not to go up to Farmer Brown's
young peach orchard. He had felt in
his bones that it was not safe, that
something dreadful would happen to
Peter. How Peter had laughed at him
and bravely started off! Why hadn't he
come home?

As he limped around, Danny talked
to himself:

" Why cannot people be content
With all the good things that are sent,
And mind their own affairs at home
Instead of going forth to roam? "

It was now the second night since
Peter Rabbit had gone away. Danny
Meadow Mouse couldn't sleep at all.
Round and round through the Old Briar-
patch he limped, and finally sat down
at the edge of it to wait and watch.
At last, just as jolly, round, red Mr.
Sun sent his first long rays of light across
the Green Meadows, Danny saw something crawling towards the Old Briar-
patch. He rubbed his eyes and looked
again. It was — no, it couldn't be —
yes, it *was* Peter Rabbit! But what was
the matter with him? Always before
Peter had come home lipperty-lipperty-
lipperty-lip, but now he was crawling,
actually *crawling!* Danny Meadow
Mouse didn't know what to make of it.

Nearer and nearer came Peter. Something was following him. No, Peter was dragging something after him. At last Peter started to crawl along one of his little private paths into the Old Briar-patch. The thing dragging behind caught in the brambles, and Peter fell headlong in the snow, too tired and worn out to move. Then Danny saw what the trouble was. A wire was fast to one of Peter's long hind legs, and to the other end of the wire was fastened part of a stake. Peter had been caught in a snare! Danny hurried over to Peter and tears stood in his eyes.

"Poor Peter Rabbit! Oh, I'm so sorry, Peter!" he whispered.

XVIII

DANNY MEADOW MOUSE RETURNS A KINDNESS

THERE Peter Rabbit lay. He had dragged that piece of stake a long way, a very long way, indeed. But now he could drag it no farther, for it had caught in the bramble bushes. So Peter just dropped on the snow and cried. Yes, Sir, he cried! You see he was so tired and worn out and frightened, and his leg was so stiff and sore and hurt him so! And then it was so dreadful to actually get home and be stopped right on your very own door-step. So Peter just lay there and cried. Just supposing old Granny Fox should come poking around and find Peter caught that way! All she would have to do would be to get hold of that hateful stake caught in the bramble bushes and pull Peter out where she could get him. Do you wonder that Peter cried?

By and by he became aware that some one was wiping away his tears. It was Danny Meadow Mouse. And Danny was singing in a funny little voice. Pretty soon Peter stopped crying and listened, and this is what he heard:

> " Isn't any use to cry!
>   Not a bit! Not a bit!
>   Wipe your eyes and wipe 'em dry!
>   Use your wit! Use your wit!
>   Just remember that to-morrow
>   Never brings a single sorrow.
>   Yesterday has gone forever
>   And to-morrow gets here never.
>   Chase your worries all away;
>   Nothing's worse than just to-day."

Peter smiled in spite of himself.

" That's right! That's right! Smile

away, Peter Rabbit. Smile away! Your troubles, Sir, are all to-day. And between you and me, I don't believe they are so bad as you think they are. Now you lie still just where you are, while I go see what can be done."

With that off whisked Danny Meadow Mouse as spry as you please, in spite of his lame leg, and in a few minutes Peter knew by little twitches of the wire on his leg that Danny was doing something at the other end. He was. Danny Meadow Mouse had set out to gnaw that piece of stake all to splinters. So there he sat and gnawed and gnawed and gnawed. Jolly, round, red Mr. Sun climbed higher and higher in the sky, and Danny Meadow Mouse grew hungry, but still he kept right on gnawing at that bothersome stake.

By and by, happening to look across the snow-covered Green Meadows, he

saw something that made his heart
jump. It was Farmer Brown's boy
coming straight over towards the dear
Old Briar-patch. Danny didn't say a
word to Peter Rabbit, but gnawed faster
than ever.

Farmer Brown's boy was almost there
when Danny stopped gnawing. There
was only a tiny bit of the stake left now,
and Danny hurried to tell Peter Rabbit
that there was nothing to stop him now
from going to his most secret retreat in
the very heart of the Old Briar-patch.
While Peter slowly dragged his way
along, Danny trotted behind to see that
the wire did not catch on the bushes.
They had safely reached Peter Rabbit's
secretest retreat when Farmer Brown's
boy came up to the edge of the dear
Old Briar-patch.

" So this is where that rabbit that
killed our peach-tree lives! " said he.

"We'll try a few snares and put you out of mischief."

And for the rest of the afternoon Farmer Brown's boy was very busy around the edge of the Old Briar-patch.

XIX

PETER RABBIT AND DANNY MEADOW MOUSE LIVE HIGH

PETER RABBIT sat in his secret-est place in the dear Old Briar-patch with one of his long hind legs all swelled up and terribly sore because of the fine wire fast around it and cutting into it. He could hear Farmer Brown's boy going around on the edge of the dear Old Briar-patch and stopping every little while to do something. In spite of his pain, Peter was curious. Finally he called Danny Meadow Mouse.

" Danny, you are small and can keep out of sight easier than I can. Go as near as ever you dare to Farmer Brown's boy and find out what he is doing," said Peter Rabbit.

So Danny Meadow Mouse crept out as near to Farmer Brown's boy as ever he dared and studied and studied to make out what Farmer Brown's boy was doing. By and by he returned to Peter Rabbit.

" I don't know what he's doing, Peter, but he's putting something in every one of your private little paths leading in from the Green Meadows."

" Ha! " said Peter Rabbit.

" There are little loops of that queer stuff you've got hanging to your leg, Peter," continued Danny Meadow Mouse.

" Just so! " said Peter Rabbit.

" And he's put cabbage leaves and pieces of apple all around," said Danny.

" We must be careful! " said Peter Rabbit.

Peter's leg was in a very bad way, indeed, and Peter suffered a great deal of pain. The worst of it was, he didn't know how to get off the wire that was cutting into it so. He had tried to cut the wire with his big teeth, but he couldn't do it. Danny Meadow Mouse had tried and tried to gnaw the wire, but it wasn't of the least bit of use. But Danny wasn't easily discouraged, and he kept working and working at it. Once he thought he felt it slip a little. He said nothing, but kept right on working. Pretty soon he was sure that it slipped. He went right on working harder than ever. By and by he had it so loose that he slipped it right off of Peter's leg, and Peter didn't know anything about it. You see, that cruel wire snare had been so tight that Peter didn't have any feeling except of pain left in his leg, and so when Danny Meadow Mouse pulled

the cruel wire snare off, Peter didn't
know it until Danny held it up in front
of him.

My, how thankful Peter was, and
how he did thank Danny Meadow
Mouse! But Danny said that it was
nothing at all, just nothing at all, and
that he owed more than that to Peter
Rabbit for being so good to him and
letting him live in the dear Old Briar-
patch.

It was a long time before Peter could
hop as he used to, but after the first
day he managed to get around. He
found that Farmer Brown's boy had
spread those miserable wire snares in
every one of his private little paths.
But Peter knew what they were now.
He showed Danny Meadow Mouse how
he, because he was so small, could safely
run about among the snares and steal
all the cabbage leaves and apples which

Farmer Brown's boy had put there for bait.

Danny Meadow Mouse thought this great fun and a great joke on Farmer Brown's boy. So every day he stole the bait, and he and Peter Rabbit lived high while Peter's leg was getting well. And all the time Farmer Brown's boy wondered and wondered why he couldn't catch Peter Rabbit.

XX

TIMID DANNY MEADOW MOUSE

DANNY MEADOW MOUSE is timid. Everybody says so, and what everybody says ought to be so. But just as anybody can make a mistake sometimes, so can everybody. Still, in this case, it is quite likely that everybody is right. Danny Meadow Mouse *is* timid. Ask Peter Rabbit. Ask Sammy Jay. Ask Striped Chipmunk. They will all tell you the same thing. Sammy Jay might even tell you that Danny is afraid of his own shadow, or that he tries to run away from his own tail. Of course this isn't true. Sammy Jay likes to say

mean things. It isn't fair to Danny
Meadow Mouse to believe what Sammy
Jay says.

But the fact is Danny certainly is
timid. More than this, he isn't ashamed
of it — not the least little bit.

"You see, it's this way," said Danny,
as he sat on his door-step one sunny
morning talking to his friend, old Mr.
Toad. "If I weren't afraid, I wouldn't
be all the time watching out, and if I
weren't all the time watching out, I
wouldn't have any more chance than
that foolish red ant running across in
front of you."

Old Mr. Toad looked where Danny
was pointing, and his tongue darted out
and back again so quickly that Danny
wasn't sure that he saw it at all, but
when he looked for the ant it was nowhere to be seen, and there was a satisfied twinkle in Mr. Toad's eyes. There

was an answering twinkle in Danny's own eyes as he continued.

"No, Sir," said he, "I wouldn't stand a particle more chance than that foolish ant did. Now if I were big and strong, like Old Man Coyote, or had swift wings, like Skimmer the Swallow, or were so homely and ugly looking that no one wanted me, like — like — " Danny hesitated and then finished rather lamely, "like some folks I know, I suppose I wouldn't be afraid."

Old Mr. Toad looked up sharply when Danny mentioned homely and ugly looking people, but Danny was gazing far out across the Green Meadows and looked so innocent that Mr. Toad concluded that he couldn't have had him in mind.

"Well," said he, thoughtfully scratching his nose, "I suppose you may be right, but for my part fear seems a

very foolish thing. Now, I don't know
what it is. I mind my own business,
and no one ever bothers me. I should
think it would be a very uncomfortable
feeling."

"It is," replied Danny, "but, as I said
before, it is a very good thing to keep one
on guard when there are so many watching for one as there are for me. Now
there's Mr. Blacksnake and —"

"Where?" exclaimed old Mr. Toad,
turning as pale as a Toad can turn, and
looking uneasily and anxiously in every
direction.

Danny turned his head to hide a smile.
If old Mr. Toad wasn't showing fear, no
one ever did. "Oh," said he, "I didn't
mean that he is anywhere around here
now. What I was going to say was that
there is Mr. Blacksnake and Granny
Fox and Reddy Fox and Redtail the
Hawk and Hooty the Owl and others I

might name, always watching for a
chance to make a dinner from poor little
me. Do you wonder that I am afraid
most of the time? "

"No," replied old Mr. Toad. "No,
I don't wonder that you are afraid. It
must be dreadful to feel hungry eyes are
watching for you every minute of the
day and night, too."

"Oh, it's not so bad," replied Danny.
"It's rather exciting. Besides, it keeps
my wits sharp all the time. I am afraid
I should find life very dull indeed if, like
you, I feared nothing and nobody. By
the way, see how queerly that grass is
moving over there. It looks as if Mr.
Blacksnake — Why, Mr. Toad, where
are you going in such a hurry? "

"I've just remembered an important
engagement with my cousin, Grandfather Frog, at the Smiling Pool," shouted
old Mr. Toad over his shoulder, as he

hurried so that he fell over his own
feet.

Danny chuckled as he sat alone on his
door-step. "Oh, no, old Mr. Toad doesn't
know what fear is!" said he. "Funny
how some people won't admit what
everybody can see for themselves. Now,
I *am* afraid, and I'm willing to say so."

XXI

AN EXCITING DAY FOR DANNY MEADOW MOUSE

DANNY MEADOW MOUSE started along one of his private little paths very early one morning. He was on his way to get a supply of a certain kind of grass-seed of which he is very fond. He had been thinking about that seed for some time and waiting for it to get ripe. Now it was just right, as he had found out the day before by a visit to the place where this particular grass grew. The only trouble was it grew a long way from Danny's home, and to reach it he had to cross an open place where the grass was so short that he couldn't make a path under it.

"I feel it in my bones that this is going to be an exciting day," said Danny to himself as he trotted along. "I suppose that if I were really wise, I would stay nearer home and do without that nice seed. But nothing is really worth having unless it is worth working for, and that seed will taste all the better if I have hard work getting it."

So he trotted along his private little path, his ears wide open, and his eyes wide open, and his little nose carefully testing every Merry Little Breeze who happened along for any scent of danger which it might carry. Most of all he depended upon his ears, for the grass was so tall that he couldn't see over it, even when he sat up. He had gone only a little way when he thought he heard a queer rustling behind him. He stopped to listen. There it was again, and it certainly was right in the path be-

hind him! He didn't need to be told
who was making it. There was only
one who could make such a sound as
that — Mr. Blacksnake.

Now Danny can run very fast along
his private little paths, but he knew
that Mr. Blacksnake could run faster.
"If my legs can't save me, my wits
must," thought Danny as he started to
run as fast as ever he could. "I must
reach that fallen old hollow fence-
post."

He was almost out of breath when he
reached the post and scurried into the
open end. He knew by the sound of the
rustling that Mr. Blacksnake was right
at his heels. Now the old post was
hollow its whole length, but half-way
there was an old knot-hole just big
enough for Danny to squeeze through.
Mr. Blacksnake didn't know anything
about that hole, and because it was dark

inside the old post, he didn't see Danny
pop through it. Danny ran back along
the top of the log and was just in time
to see the tip of Mr. Blacksnake's tail
disappear inside. Then what do you
think Danny did? Why, he followed
Mr. Blacksnake right into the old post,
but in doing it he didn't make the least
little bit of noise.

Mr. Blacksnake kept right on through
the old post and out the other end, for
he was sure that that was the way
Danny had gone. He kept right on
along the little path. Now Danny knew
that he wouldn't go very far before he
found out that he had been fooled, and
of course he would come back. So
Danny waited only long enough to get
his breath and then ran back along the
path to where another little path
branched off. For just a minute he
paused.

"If Mr. Blacksnake follows me, he will be sure to think that of course I have taken this other little path," thought Danny, "so I won't do it."

Then he ran harder than ever, until he came to a place where two little paths branched off, one to the right and one to the left. He took the latter and scampered on, sure that by this time Mr. Blacksnake would be so badly fooled that he would give up the chase. And Danny was right.

"Brains are better far than speed
   As wise men long ago agreed,"

said Danny, as he trotted on his way for the grass-seed he liked so well. "I felt it in my bones that this would be an exciting day. I wonder what next."

XXII

WHAT HAPPENED NEXT TO DANNY MEADOW MOUSE

DANNY is so used to narrow escapes that he doesn't waste any time thinking about them. He didn't this time. " He who tries to look two ways at once is pretty sure to see nothing," says Danny, and he knew that if he thought too much about the things that had already happened, he couldn't keep a sharp watch for the things that might happen.

Nothing more happened as he hurried along his private little path to the edge of a great patch of grass so short that he couldn't hide under it. He had got to cross this, and all the way he would be in plain sight of any one who happened to be near. Very cautiously he peeped out and looked this way and looked that way, not forgetting to look up in the sky. He could see no one anywhere. Drawing a long breath, Danny started across the open place as fast as his short legs could take him.

Now all the time, Redtail the Hawk had been sitting in a tree some distance away, sitting so still that he looked like a part of the tree itself. That is why Danny hadn't seen him. But Redtail saw Danny the instant he started across the open place, for Redtail's eyes are very keen, and he can see a great distance. With a satisfied chuckle, he spread his broad wings and started after Danny.

Just about half-way to the safety of the long grass on the other side, Danny gave a hurried look behind him, and his heart seemed to jump right into his mouth, for there was Redtail with his cruel claws already set to seize him! Danny gave a frightened squeak, for he thought that surely this time he would be caught. But he didn't mean to give up without trying to escape. Three jumps ahead of him was a queer looking thing. He didn't know what it was, but if there was a hole in it he might yet fool Redtail.

One jump! Would he be able to reach it? Two jumps! There *was* a hole in it! Three jumps! With another frightened squeak, Danny dived into the opening just in time. And what do you think he was in? Why, an old tomato can Farmer Brown's boy had once used to carry bait in when he went fishing at the Smiling Pool. He had dropped it there on his way home.

Redtail screamed with rage and dis-

appointment as he struck the old can
with his great claws. He had been sure,
very sure of Danny Meadow Mouse this
time! He tried to pick the can up, but
he couldn't get hold of it. It just rolled
away from him every time, try as he
would. Finally, in disgust, he gave up
and flew back to the tree from which he
had first seen Danny.

Of course Danny had been terribly
frightened when the can rolled, and by
the noise the claws of Redtail made
when they struck his queer hiding-place.
But he wisely decided that the best
thing he could do was to stay there for a
while. And it was very fortunate that he
did so, as he was very soon to find out.

XXIII

DANNY MEADOW MOUSE had sat perfectly still for a long time inside the old tomato can in which he had found a refuge from Redtail the Hawk. He didn't dare so much as put his head out for a look around, lest Redtail should be circling overhead ready to pounce on him.

"If I stay here long enough, he'll get tired and go away, if he hasn't already," thought Danny. "This has been a pretty exciting morning so far, and I find that I am a little tired. I may as well take a nap while I am waiting to make sure that the way is clear."

With that Danny curled up in the

old tomato can. But it wasn't meant
that Danny should have that nap. He
had closed his eyes, but his ears were
still open, and presently he heard soft
footsteps drawing near. His eyes flew
open, and he forgot all about sleep, you
may be sure, for those footsteps sounded
familiar. They sounded to Danny very,
very much like the footsteps of — whom
do you think? Why, Reddy Fox!
Danny's heart began to beat faster as
he listened. Could it be? He didn't
dare peep out. Presently a little whiff
of scent blew into the old tomato can.
Then Danny knew — it *was* Reddy Fox.

"Oh, dear! I hope he doesn't find
that I am in here!" thought Danny.
"I wonder what under the sun has
brought him up here just now."

If the truth were to be known, it was
curiosity that had brought Reddy up
there. Reddy had been hunting for his

breakfast some distance away on the
Green Meadows when Redtail the Hawk
had tried so hard to catch Danny
Meadow Mouse. Reddy's sharp eyes
had seen Redtail the minute he left the
tree in pursuit of Danny, and he had
known by the way Redtail flew that he
saw something he wanted to catch.
He had watched Redtail swoop down
and had heard his scream of rage when
he missed Danny because Danny had
dodged into the old tomato can. He
had seen Redtail strike and strike again
at something on the ground, and finally
fly off in disgust with empty claws.

"Now, I wonder what it was Redtail
was after and why he didn't get it,"
thought Reddy. "He acts terribly put
out and disappointed. I believe I'll go
over there and find out."

Off he started at a smart trot towards
the patch of short grass where he had

seen Redtail the Hawk striking at something on the ground. As he drew near, he crept very softly until he reached the very edge of the open patch. There he stopped and looked sharply all over it. There was nothing to be seen but an old tomato can. Reddy had seen it many times before.

" Now what under the sun could Redtail have been after here?" thought Reddy. " The grass isn't long enough for a grasshopper to hide in, and yet Redtail didn't get what he was after. It's very queer. It certainly is very queer."

He trotted out and began to run back and forth with his nose to the ground, hoping that his nose would tell him what his eyes couldn't. Back and forth, back and forth he ran, and then suddenly he stopped.

" Ha! " exclaimed Reddy. He had

found the scent left by Danny Meadow
Mouse when he ran across towards the
old tomato can. Right up to the old
can Reddy's nose led him. He hopped
over the old can, but on the other side
he could find no scent of Danny Meadow
Mouse. In a flash he understood, and a
gleam of satisfaction shone in his yellow
eyes as he turned back to the old can.
He knew that Danny must be hiding in
there.

" I've got you this time! " he snarled,
as he sniffed at the opening in the end
of the can.

XXIV

REDDY FOX LOSES HIS TEMPER

REDDY FOX had caught Danny Meadow Mouse, and yet he hadn't caught him. He had found Danny hiding in the old tomato can, and it didn't enter Reddy's head that he couldn't get Danny out when he wanted to. He was in no hurry. He had had a pretty good breakfast of grasshoppers, and so he thought he would torment Danny a while before gobbling him up. He lay down so that he could peep in at the open end of the old can and see Danny trying to make himself as small as possible at the other end. Reddy grinned until he showed

all his long teeth. Reddy always is a
bully, especially when his victim is a
great deal smaller and weaker than
himself.

"I've got you this time, Mr. Smarty,
haven't I?" taunted Reddy.

Danny didn't say anything.

"You think you've been very clever
because you have fooled me two or three
times, don't you? Well, this time I've
got you where your tricks won't work,"
continued Reddy, "so what are you
going to do about it?"

Danny didn't answer. The fact is, he
was too frightened to answer. Besides,
he didn't know what he could do. So
he just kept still, but his bright eyes
never once left Reddy's cruel face. For
all his fright, Danny was doing some
hard thinking. He had been in tight
places before and had learned never to
give up hope. Something might hap-

pen to frighten Reddy away. Anyway,
Reddy had got to get him out of that
old can before he would admit that he
was really caught.

For a long time Reddy lay there
licking his chops and saying all the
things he could think of to frighten poor
Danny Meadow Mouse. At last he
grew tired of this and made up his mind
that it was time to end it and Danny
Meadow Mouse at the same time. He
thrust his sharp nose in at the opening
in the end of the old can, but the opening was too small for him to get more
than his nose in, and he only scratched
it on the sharp edges without so much
as touching Danny.

" I'll pull you out," said Reddy and
thrust in one black paw.

Danny promptly bit it so hard that
Reddy yelped with pain and pulled it
out in a hurry. Presently he tried again

with the other paw. Danny bit this
one harder still, and Reddy danced with
pain and anger. Then he lost his temper completely, a very foolish thing to
do, as it always is. He hit the old can,
and away it rolled with Danny Meadow
Mouse inside. This seemed to make
Reddy angrier than ever. He sprang
after it and hit it again. Then he batted
it first this way and then that way,
growing angrier and angrier. And all
the time Danny Meadow Mouse managed to keep inside, although he got a
terrible shaking up.

Back and forth across the patch of
short grass Reddy knocked the old can,
and he was in such a rage that he didn't
notice where he was knocking it to.
Finally he sent it spinning into the
long grass on the far side of the open
patch, close to one of Danny's private
little paths. Like a flash Danny was

out and scurrying along the little path.
He dodged into another and presently
into a third, which brought him to a
tangle of barbed wire left there by
Farmer Brown when he had built a
new fence. Under this he was safe.

" Phew! " exclaimed Danny, breath-
ing very hard. " That was the narrow-
est escape yet! But I guess I'll get that
special grass-seed I started out for, after
all."

And he did, while to this day Reddy
Fox wonders how Danny got out of the
old tomato can without him knowing
it.

> And so you see what temper does
> For those who give it rein;
> It cheats them of the very thing
> They seek so hard to gain.

Danny has had many more adventures, but there isn't room to tell about
them here. Besides Grandfather Frog

is anxious that you should hear about the queer things that have happened to him. They are told in the next book.